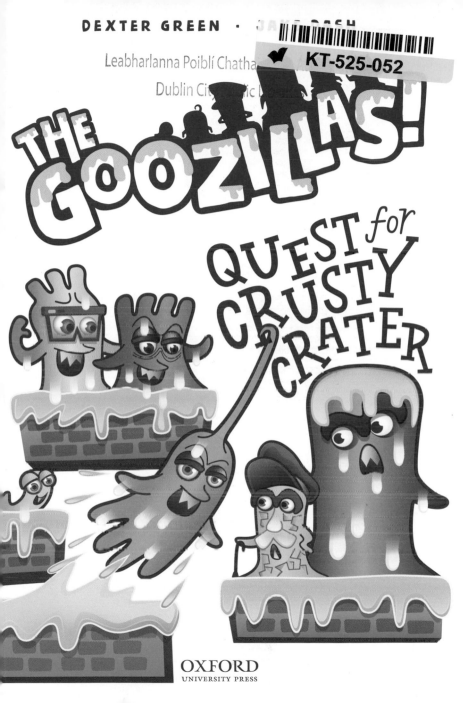

DEXTER GREEN · JANE PASH

THE GOOZILLAS!

QUEST for CRUSTY CRATER

OXFORD
UNIVERSITY PRESS

GOOEY AND GREEN, THE ULTIMATE TEAM! MEET THE GOOZILLAS!

Can the **EVIL**
CKLIES be defeated?

'My favourite Goozilla is **GLOOP**,
I like his little head swirl, he is
AWESOME!'

ISLA

Prepare for the
SLIMIEST
ADVENTURE ever!

ke **ATISHOO**
because he's the silliest
of the Goozillas!'

CHLOE

OXFORD
UNIVERSITY PRESS

Great Clarendon Street, Oxford OX2 6DP

Oxford University Press is a department of the University of Oxford.
It furthers the University's objective of excellence in research, scholarship,
and education by publishing worldwide. Oxford is a registered trade mark
of Oxford University Press in the UK and in certain other countries

Copyright © Barry Hutchison and Oxford University Press 2018
Illustrations © chris@kja-artists 2018

The moral rights of the author have been asserted

Database right Oxford University Press (maker)

First published 2018

British Library Cataloguing in Publication Data

Data available

ISBN: 978-0-19-276378-5

1 3 5 7 9 10 8 6 4 2

Printed in China

Paper used in the production of this book is a natural,
recyclable product made from wood grown in sustainable forests.
The manufacturing process conforms to the environmental
regulations of the country of origin.

WELCOME TO THE
WORLD OF
SLIME

SIX *AWESOME* LEVELS TO EXPLORE

Enter a team into the great **GUNGE GAMES**. There are loads of slimy sports to take part in, and win!

Leap from platform to platform, to reach the dizzying heights of the **CRUSTY CRATER**. Whatever you do, don't look down.

It's a dash to the finish line as you speed around this ultimate racing circuit. Can you reach **SLIME CENTRAL** in one piece?

Battle it out in a mission to capture the **FUNGUS FORT**. Beware: you'll need more than ninja skills to defeat the enemies on this level.

Can you escape from the **MONSTROUS MAZE**? Just when you think you're on the right track, the ghostly Gools will be ready to attack.

Dare you enter the dungeon of slime? Watch your step or you just might end up stuck in the **BOG OF BEASTS**!

THE STORY SO FAR

After accidentally **sneezing** all over his tablet computer, Max found himself whisked inside his favourite app, **WORLD OF SLIME**, where he came face-to-face with the Goozillas, a group of green, **slimy** creatures he had created in the game.

When Max discovered that his **sneeze** had destroyed the **GOLDEN GLOB**—a magical artefact that keeps the **WORLD OF SLIME** goo flowing—and that without it the Goozillas' volcano home would completely dry out, he teamed up with his icky new

friends and set off to
retrieve all the missing pieces,
hoping to fix the **GOLDEN GLOB**
and bring back the **slime**.

Unfortunately, a group of cutesy-wootsy,
sickly-sweet animals from the neighbouring
World of Pets app—fed up of having to dress up
and play on rainbows all the time—decided they
were going to move in to the **slime** volcano.

If the evil Bubble Kitten and her band of
Sicklies get the **GOLDEN GLOB** pieces, then it's
the end for the Goozillas, and so thanks to that
one fateful **sneeze**, Max has found himself in
a frantic race not just to save his new friends,
but all of **WORLD OF SLIME** itself!

EET THE GOOZILLAS

JOE

The joker of the gang. Equipped with special slime-seeking gadget glasses.

GLOOP

The first Goozilla that Max created, and his favourite by far.

ATISHOO

A teeny, baby Goozilla, with an enormous sneeze.

GUNK

A mean, green, fighting machine!

BIG BLOB

Supersized, and super strong, but definitely not super smart.

CAPTAIN CRUST

Old, crusty, and in command.

and the sicklies

BUBBLE KITTEN

The evil leader of the Sicklies. She can blow bubble kisses to trap her enemies.

SUGAR PAWS PUPPY

Bubble Kitten's faithful sidekick. His sticky paw prints will stop you in your tracks.

GLITTER CHICK

Watch out for her eggs-plosive glitterbomb eggs.

DREAMY BUNNY

Beware of her powerful hypnotic gaze.

SQUEAKY GUINEA PIG

His supersonic screech will leave your ears ringing.

SCAMPY HAMSTER

The ultimate kickass, street-fighting, rodent.

CHAPTER ONE

THE LAVA FLOOR

Max's little sister, Amy, stood in the middle
of the hall, wobbling slightly on a cushion.
There were six other cushions spread out
on the floor between Max and the bottom
of the stairs. When Max tried to step over
them, Amy held up a hand and screamed.

'STOP! It's lava!'

Max blinked in surprise. He had his
tablet tucked under one arm, and was
excited to go and rejoin the Goozillas in
the **WORLD OF SLIME**. He didn't have
time for Amy's silly games.

'What's lava?' he asked.

'The floor,' said Amy, dropping her voice to a whisper. 'You have to jump on the islands.'

She jumped from one cushion to another, **WOBBLED** unsteadily for a moment, then breathed a sigh of relief when she caught her balance. 'Like that.'

Max rolled his eyes and stepped over a cushion. 'Yeah, that's not going to happen,' he said. 'It's my turn with the tablet. I'm going upstairs to play.'

'Mum!' Amy cried. 'Max is walking through the lava!'

'Don't walk through the lava, Max,' replied Mum from the kitchen.

Amy stuck out her tongue, then folded her arms, smugly. 'See? Mum says you have to do it.'

Max tutted. 'Fine,' he said, stepping onto the first cushion. It was small, but thick, and **slid** sideways when Max stood on it.

'Your foot's in the lava!' Amy laughed, as Max placed a foot on the floor to steady himself. 'Now you've got to hop.'

Max stepped fully onto the floor and kicked the cushion away. 'Argh. Ouch,' he said, walking past his sister. 'It burns. It burns.'

Once past Amy, he kicked another cushion away. Amy looked down and realized she was stranded in the middle of the hall. 'Hey! Put the islands back,' she said. 'I'll be stuck!'

Max reached the bottom of the stairs and smirked at her. 'Sorry, can't hear you, I'm **DROWNING** in **LAVA**,' he said, then he took the stairs two at a time, hurried into his bedroom, and closed the door behind him.

Even with the door closed, Max could hear Amy complaining. Mum's voice came next, patient and soothing. Max heard her say something about baking, and Amy let out a **CHEER**.

'Yes!' Max whispered. Mum and Amy baking was good for two reasons. Firstly, it meant he'd have cakes to eat later. Cakes were always good, even if they did have little edible pictures of Barbie or Disney Princesses or whatever stuck to the top of them.

Secondly, and more importantly, it would mean they'd be busy for ages, which meant he wouldn't be interrupted.

Settling himself on his bed, Max turned on the tablet. A screen filled with app icons appeared and there, right in the middle, was the **WORLD OF SLIME** icon. Max glanced, just briefly, at the sickly-sweet World of Pets icon beside it, then tapped on his favourite app.

The screen changed to show the inside of the **slime VOLCANO** where the Goozillas lived. When Max saw it, he let out a little **GASP** of shock. Ever since he'd accidentally broken the **GOLDEN GLOB**, the volcano had been slowly drying up. Now, though, the **slime** looked crusty and brittle, like week-old bogies.

He and the Goozillas had found four of the six missing **GLOB** pieces, but the other two were still out there. And with the evil Bubble Kitten and her **Sicklies** after them, too, Max knew there was no time to waste.

To get inside the game, he had to **sneeze** on the screen, and he'd come prepared. With one finger, he poked a little pile of pepper up one nostril, while using a feather to tickle the other nostril.

He felt the **sneeze** building almost straight away. His head snapped back, his eyes watered, and with an

HOOO

he sprayed string wads of nose **goo** all over the screen. The snot fizzed and popped. Max looked up just as his bedroom ceiling began to loop and spin. His bed went from being solid to being **slimy**. His stomach spun, as if it was in a washing machine, and then, with a soft, squidgy **POP**, Max vanished.

CHAPTER TWO
REUNITED

With a **WHOOSH**,
Max appeared on a square platform.

A small square platform.

Right at the *edge* of a small square platform, that was floating in mid-air.

'**WAAARGH!**' Max frantically flapped his arms as he lost his balance. There was a sudden lurching feeling as he fell, plunging all the way to . . .

THONK.

He hit the ground. The platform was only thirty centimetres or so in the air, and

Max was relieved he hadn't had time to start screaming. Waving his arms around was embarrassing enough. If he'd been screaming too, he'd never have been able to live it down.

'Max!' said Gloop, oozing over to where Max had landed. Gloop was the first Goozilla Max had ever created in the game and—although he'd never tell the others—Max's favourite.

A ripple of excitement went around the rest of the **gooey** group of Goozillas, and they all hurried to greet their friend.

'Hey, Max!' said Joe, his eyes sparkling behind his gadget glasses.

'Good to see you, Max,' said tiny Atishoo. He was sitting on the head of

Big Blob, the largest Goozilla of all. Blob himself could be a bit slow at times and hadn't yet noticed Max's arrival, but he'd realize eventually.

Even the tough-talking Gunk, who rarely displayed any kind of affection, nodded and smiled as Max shook hands, received pats on the back, and was generally made to feel at home.

There was someone missing, though.
Max looked around, frowning. They were
inside another of the volcano's many
large chambers, and Max could see all
the way to the walls in every direction.
There was no sign of Captain Crust
anywhere.

'Where's the captain?' he asked.

The Goozillas' excitement faded away.
From behind Big Blob, there came a
dry, scraping sound. Max felt his jaw
drop as Captain Crust shuffled out from
behind the big Goozilla, leaning on his
SNOTSHOOTER cane for support.

'Captain Crust?' Max whispered.

The old Goozilla tried to smile, but
his **slimy** surface was so dried out his

14

mouth could barely make the shape. 'Ah, Max,' he said, in a slightly breathless wheeze. 'So good to see you.'

Max didn't need to ask what was wrong. With the **GOLDEN GLOB** destroyed, and the **slime** running out, Captain Crust was drying up. If the **slime** didn't return, the old Goozilla was done for.

'Good to see you, too,' said Max, doing his best to smile back.

'You're just in time!' said Gloop. 'We were about to start without you.'

Max frowned. 'Start what?'

Gloop pointed upwards. Max looked to where Gloop was indicating, then let out a **GASP** when he saw hundreds of platforms floating in the air above them. Some of them seemed to be fixed in place, but others moved from side to side or up and down. A few **FLICKERED** occasionally, becoming invisible for a few seconds, before appearing again.

They were all shapes and sizes, made of all sorts of materials. Some were stone, others were metal. A few were **slimy**,

while at least one looked like it was made of ice, and would be too slippery to safely jump onto.

Way, way up high, Max could see a narrow hole leading up to the level above. There were similar holes on every level, usually leading to the next chamber in the volcano. This time, though, Max could see a circle of blue sky beyond the hole.

'QUEST for CRUSTY CRATER,' he whispered, realizing what level he was on. 'This is the platform jumping game that leads to the final stage.'

'Yep!' said Joe. 'And look.'

He turned Max's head, just a little, so Max was looking slightly to the left of the hole.

There, hovering in mid-air, far from any of the platforms, was a piece of the **GOLDEN GLOB**. It shone like a tiny golden sun, casting its glow across the chamber's ceiling.

'The **GLOB** piece!' cried Max. He scrambled onto the low platform he'd fallen off, then looked back at the others. 'Come on, what are we waiting for? Let's go and get it.'

'Not so fast!'

Max spun around, then groaned. There, striding towards them, was Bubble Kitten and her **Sicklies**.

'Please, save your adoring cheers and applause,' sneered the fluffy pink cat. 'Although you should all feel free to bow, if you wish.'

'Bubble Kitten,' Gunk spat. 'Should have guessed you wouldn't be far away.'

The villain stopped. Unfortunately, her sidekick, Sugar Paws Puppy, didn't. Bubble Kitten yelped in pain as Sugar Paws stepped on her tail.

'BE CAREFUL, YOU DOLT!'

she hissed.

'Sorry, boss,' said
Sugar Paws.
The other **Sicklies**—Glitter

20

Chick, Scampy Hamster, and Squeaky Guinea Pig—fanned out behind Bubble Kitten. They all glared at Max and the Goozillas, trying to look menacing.

'I'm afraid you're not getting that **GLOB** piece,' Bubble Kitten purred. 'We are.'

'I'm pretty sure you've said that before,' Gloop snorted.

'And yet, we've got all four pieces,' Joe added.

Max nodded and folded his arms. 'First one to the top gets the **GLOB** piece,' he said. 'And we already beat you in one race.'

Bubble Kitten sneered. 'Yes. Quite,' she said. 'However, this time, I think we'll take the shortcut.'

With that, she pursed her lips and began to blow a bubble. It grew larger and larger around her and the **Sicklies** until it was big enough to fit them all inside. Then, to Max's horror, the bubble began to rise into the air, carrying Bubble Kitten and her minions up in the direction of the **GLOB** piece.

'Good luck with all that jumping,' Bubble Kitten laughed.

'I PREFER TO FLY.'

CHAPTER THREE

HEAD START

Oh no!' Max yelped. 'They're getting away.'

Joe tapped his gadget glasses, then smiled when a dotted line appeared on the lenses, showing the bubble's projected route. 'Oh, I wouldn't worry too much,' he said.

A few metres above Max's head, the bubble **THUDDED** against the underside of one of the platforms. It rolled sideways a little, then **JAMMED** itself between the first platform and the one next to it.

'Huh? What?' spluttered Bubble Kitten. She rocked violently back and forth, trying to free the bubble. The other **Sicklies** joined in, but the bubble was going nowhere. 'We're stuck! How can we be stuck?!'

Down below, Gloop grinned. 'The platforms are too close together. Your bubble won't fit through.'

'Looks like you'll have to do it the old-fashioned way, after all,' wheezed Captain Crust.

'**BAH!**' spat the cat, then she flashed her claws and the bubble vanished with a **POP**. Bubble Kitten's wide eyes went even wider. Around her, the other **Sicklies** all gasped.

'Ooh, I really didn't think that through,' Bubble Kitten said, then she screamed as she fell, before landing on a platform with a painful-sounding thump.

Bubble Kitten got to her feet, just in time for the other **Sicklies** to land on top of her. Max and the Goozillas all laughed as the wicked kitty was buried beneath a pile of fur and feathers.

'GET OFF!
GET OFF!'

she shouted, squirming out from beneath them.

Once she was free, all five **Sicklies** balanced on the narrow platform and peered at the Goozillas below.

'I don't know why you're laughing,' the cat called down.

'We're laughing at you getting flattened,' said Max.

'Yeah, it was hilarious,' giggled Gloop.

'Funny!' agreed Big Blob, who had finally caught up with what was going on.

Bubble Kitten scowled.

'Well, let's see if you find this funny. We might not be able to **FLY** up, but we've still got a head start,' she said.

The Goozillas all stopped laughing. Bubble Kitten was right. She and the Sicklies had landed on a platform several metres off the ground. It would take a good minute or so for them just to catch up.

'Oh, and one other thing,' said Bubble Kitten. She **BOUNDED** up onto Sugar Paws' head, then

BACKFLIPPED onto
the
next
platform.

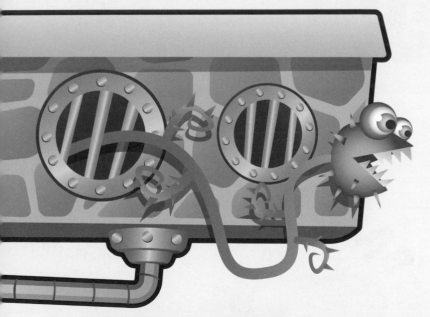

Her mouth curved into a
wide grin, and she let out a
high-pitched giggle of glee.
'Now who's laughing?' she said, as she
HURLED herself across a gap,
bounced on a platform, and landed
effortlessly on the next one.

'**Sicklies**, make sure those
slimy simpletons don't catch
up,' she commanded. 'I'll be
back with the **GLOB** piece in
no time!'

Max and the others watched Bubble
Kitten pull ahead. The other **Sicklies**
spread out onto other platforms so they
could block any Goozillas who tried to give
chase.

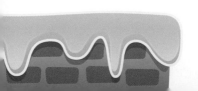

'Come on,' Max urged. 'We have to stop her.'

'But the **Sicklies** are blocking the way,' Gloop pointed out.

'There are hundreds of platforms,' said Max. 'And that means hundreds of routes to the top. They can't block all of them!'

He stepped to the edge of the platform he was on, took a deep breath, and **JUMPED**. The world seemed to hold its breath for a moment, before he landed safely on the next square. Behind him, the others clambered up onto low platforms.

Well, not all the others. Captain Crust

hung back, his moustache drooping. 'You chaps go on without me,' he said. 'I'm afraid I'm not up to jumping around all over the place these days.'

Max hesitated. 'But . . .'

The captain forced another smile. 'Oh, don't worry about me, Max. Just get the **GLOB** piece.'

Max nodded. 'We will.'

'Good show. I'll do my best to direct you from down here, if I can. Good luck!'

'They'll need more than luck!' screeched a voice from above. Squeaky Guinea Pig leaned over the edge of a platform, glaring down.

The guinea pig opened his mouth
and drew in a deep breath. Max covered
his ears, bracing himself for the
soundwave attack.

U B.

A sticky wad of **goo** streaked upwards, shot into Squeaky's mouth, and then hit the back of his throat. The villain's deafening squeak was replaced by a lot of coughing and choking.

Max looked down to find Captain Crust peering along the barrel of his **SNOTSHOOTER** cane. The old Goozilla winked. 'Like I say, I'll help where I can,' he said.

Max nodded. 'Thanks, Captain,' he said, then he looked up to the next platform, bent his knees, and **JUMPED**.

CHAPTER FOUR

DON'T LOOK DOWN

The first few platforms were easy. Max hopped across the gaps, growing more confident with each one. Captain Crust **SHOUTED** directions from below, guiding him towards platforms that led him away from the waiting Sicklies.

One platform back, Gloop and Joe were jumping and landing at exactly the same time, while Gunk hurried along behind them. Big Blob easily stepped from one platform to the next, but had to duck to avoid the ones floating above his head, which slowed him down. Atishoo also crouched low on the big Goozilla's head to avoid being squished.

Bubble Kitten was still well ahead, but the further she got, the more difficult the course became, and she was moving more slowly now. She was no longer **FLIPPING** and **BOUNDING** from platform to platform, and was carefully picking the safest route. Max felt a surge of hope. Maybe they could still catch her, after all.

Of course, the other Sicklies were still waiting above. Max had picked a route that he hoped would avoid them, but they'd now moved to try to block him and the Goozillas again.

Still, he would deal with them when he had to. Right now, he had to concentrate on jumping.

He *LEAPED* for the next platform. It was slightly further away than the last few, and he only just made it. Max landed with his heels sticking out over the ledge, and teetered there for a few seconds, his arms o u t s t r e t c h e d as he tried to stay upright.

Almost cheering with relief, Max managed to take a step forwards to safety. 'Be careful of that jump, guys,' he warned, turning to look back at the others.

And that was when Max made his big mistake.

He
looked
down.

They had only been jumping for a few minutes, but already the ground seemed to be a very long way away. From up here, Captain Crust looked like he was challenging Atishoo for the title of World's Smallest Goozilla.

Max's stomach FLIPPED and his blood ran cold. He tried to take a deep breath, but his lungs had gone tight, forcing all the air out of him.

'Are you OK, Max?' asked Gloop from a few platforms behind. He and Joe both jumped and landed on the platform closest to Max's. 'You've gone all pale.'

Max tried to speak, but his voice came out like a dry croak. 'I'm f-fine,' he whispered, then he pointed down. 'Just didn't r-realize how high it was.'

Joe and Gloop both frowned, then peered over the edge. They quickly leaned back again, their eyes going **WIDE**.

'URK!'

said Joe.

'Ooh. Yeah,' said Gloop. 'It is pretty high, isn't it? Probably shouldn't look down again.'

Joe and Max both nodded in agreement. 'Good idea,' said Max. He shuffled around on the spot, so he was facing the front again. His legs had gone all **rubbery** and **wobbly**, and he wondered if this was what it felt like to be a Goozilla.

Max gritted his teeth, summoning all his courage as he looked over to the next platform. 'You can do this,' he muttered to himself. 'You can do this.'

Swinging his arms back, Max *THREW*

himself across the gap. He resisted the urge to look down as he sailed through the air towards the rectangular platform. He landed awkwardly and stumbled forwards. Behind him, Joe and Gloop both cried out in fright.

'MAX!'

Dropping low, Max managed to stop himself running right over the edge. Phew! That was too close.

Turning, Max waved back at his worried friends. 'It's OK. I made it,' he said. 'I'm safe.'

And then, before Max could say any more, the platform beneath him disappeared, and he found himself standing on nothing, gazing down at the ground far, far below.

'Uh-oh,' Max whimpered. 'Not good.'

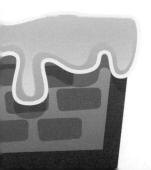

CHAPTER FIVE

NEW ARRIVAL

'Quick, Max, grab my arm!' said Joe. He and Gloop were stretching across the gap to where Max was standing on nothing but air. 'Before you . . . fall?'

But Max wasn't falling. He should have been falling—there was nothing beneath him, after all—but he wasn't.

Carefully, Max lifted one foot, then brought it back down again. The bottom of his shoe gave a reassuring **THUNK**. 'The platform's still there,' Max said. 'Just invisible.'

He shuffled very slowly forwards until

he felt his toes slide off the edge, then he bent his knees and jumped.

As soon as Max's feet touched down on the next platform, the invisible one reappeared. 'It's a trick, that's all,' Max said. 'Nothing to worry about.'

He turned to continue, then instinctively caught what he thought was a ball that came flying towards him. It wasn't until he was holding it in his hands that he realized it wasn't a ball at all.

It was an egg. A shiny, glittery egg. If Max listened very carefully, he could just hear something inside the egg going **TICK-TICK-TICK** like a clock.

On one of the platforms further ahead, Glitter Chick clucked with amusement.

Up above, Glitter Chick
watched, her **sparkly** yellow
feathers rippling as her
laughter **BOOMED** around
the cavern.

'TICK,
TOCK,
TICK, TOCK,'

she called.

'WHO'S IT
GOING
TO BE?'

Gunk looked at the egg, then he spun and hurled it back towards Big Blob a few platforms behind. 'Blob, right hook!' he instructed.

As the explosive flew towards him, the giant Goozilla swung an arm the size of a small tree trunk.

It connected hard with the egg, and Gunk, Joe, Gloop, and Max all ducked as the bomb **WHIZZED** over their heads, and back in the direction it had come from.

Glitter Chick stopped laughing.

'Ooh, this is gonna hurt,' she grunted,

then the egg went **BOOM**, knocking her from the platform. She plunged to the ground, flapping her stumpy little wings, her feathers black and scorched.

With a **THUD**, she hit the ground, then lay there, groaning, as Captain Crust trained his weapon on her.

'Freeze, you feathery fiend,' the captain warned. High above them, Max and the others all whooped and cheered in delight.

Their celebrations were cut short, though.

'**Hiiii-ya!**' cried Scampy Hamster, taking aim with three throwing stars.

'You may have defeated Glitter Chick, but you don't stand a chance against my—'

A thick, **gooey** wad of **slime** hit the hamster at high speed. 'Don't speak too soon, bub,' said Gunk. He opened fire again, and two more **goo** balls slammed into Scampy, forcing him backwards towards the edge.

'EEK! OW! CUT IT OUT!' Scampy wailed, before he lost his footing, toppled backwards, and—after a long fall and a painful-sounding **BUMP**—joined Glitter Chick down on the ground.

'Nice shooting, Gunk!' Max cheered.

Gunk spun his gun around and blew on the barrel. 'Yeah,' he said. 'I know.'

They carried on up the platforms, Max leading the way. Sugar Paws Puppy was eight or nine platforms ahead. He looked back and stuck his floppy tongue out at them.

'Haha, slow coaches. You'll never catch me!' he said. Then the platform beneath him lit up with an electric-blue glow, and all Sugar Paws' fur stood on end.

For a moment, Max could see the dog's skeleton flickering inside his body, then the platform stopped glowing.

The air was filled with the smell of burning hair. Sugar Paws blinked slowly, said, 'Ow,' very quietly under his breath, then toppled backwards off the platform.

He landed, quite heavily, on top of Glitter Chick and Scampy. They were too far away for Max to make out exactly what they were saying, but he could tell they weren't happy.

'Electric platforms ahead,' Max warned, pressing on. **'BE CAREFUL!'**

The other Goozillas followed. At the back of the line, Big Blob was starting to close the gap. The platforms were spaced further apart now, giving him more room to move between them.

Big Blob and Atishoo had almost caught up with Gunk when Blob heard a sound behind him. It was a strange, boingy sort of sound, like someone bouncing on a spring.

'Hey, what's that?' asked Atishoo from the top of his head. They both turned to see something small, white, and fluffy springing up the platforms behind them. It had big feet, a cotton-ball tail, and the longest, floppiest ears either Goozilla had ever seen.

Its wide eyes **glittered** and **shone** in that cutesy way that only a **Sicklies'** eyes did. Another of Bubble Kitten's minions had arrived from **World of Pets!**

Atishoo was about to shout and warn the others, but there was something about the bunny's eyes that made him stop. The big, wide pupils swirled, around and around and around. Each one was a little pink and purple spiral, and Atishoo suddenly found he couldn't look away from them.

'HELLO, GOOZILLAS,' said the rabbit, in a voice as smooth as chocolate.

'GAZE INTO THE EYES OF DREAMY BUNNY. YOU ARE BOTH UNDER MY COMMAND.'

Atishoo and Big Blob spoke at the same time.

'**We are both under your command.**'

'EXCELLENT,' said Dreamy Bunny, her eyes spinning *FASTER* and *FASTER*. 'NOW, HERE'S WHAT I WANT YOU TO DO . . .'

CHAPTER SIX

FRIEND TO FOE

'Bubble Kitten's taken a wrong turn!' Joe cried. He was looking up at the clambering cat high above. She had turned around, and was making her way across to another series of platforms. 'She can't reach the **GLOB** piece that way, so she's had to turn back!'

'That's the best news I've heard all day,' called Gunk, right before Atishoo slammed into him from behind, sending him stumbling over the edge.

Gunk and Atishoo fell together, tumbling end over end through the air.

They bounced off a platform, rolled sideways, and fell all the way to the floor.

Gunk complained the whole way down. 'What was that for? Have you lost your mind?'

Atishoo, meanwhile, just stared, his little eyes swirling around and around.

'Must stop the Goozillas,' he said. **'The Sicklies must get the GLOB piece.'**

'What are you talking about?' Gunk demanded, then he and Atishoo both hit the floor with a **SPLAT**.

High above, Max, Gloop, and Joe watched the two Goozillas fall. Max breathed a sigh of relief when he saw them squidging back into their normal shapes down below. 'What was that about?' he wondered.

'I'm not sure,' replied Joe, 'but I think something's wrong with Big Blob. Look!'

Sure enough, Big Blob was not his usual slightly confused-looking self. His eyes were now swirling pink spirals, and he stood perfectly still, swaying gently from side to side a few platforms behind.

'Blob, are you OK?' Gloop asked.

Bubble Kitten's voice came down from on high. 'He won't answer. You see, your oafish friend there has met the latest addition to the **Sicklies**,' she cackled. 'Dreamy Bunny, take a bow!'

A little white rabbit hopped out from behind Big Blob. She lowered her head and bowed, which made her ears touch the platform. When she straightened up, her eyes were swirling almost exactly like Big Blob's.

'**BIG BLOB**,' said Dreamy Bunny, in her sing-song voice. She raised a paw and pointed to Max and the others. '**DESTROY THEM. DESTROY MAX AND THE GOOZILLAS.**'

For a moment, Big Blob didn't respond. But then his **slimy** eyebrows furrowed and his mouth pulled into an angry snarl.

'Must destroy Max
and the Goozillas,'

he said.

The platform beneath him shook as he launched himself forwards, his arms outstretched in front of him.

'Uh-oh,' said Gloop.

'This is bad,' said Joe.

'Should we run?' asked Max. Big Blob let out a furious roar as he bounded across another set of platforms. 'Yes. Yes, I think we should probably run.'

The three friends turned and hurled themselves onwards, Max still just one jump ahead of the others.

'**FASTER, BIG BLOB!**' urged Dreamy Bunny. 'Don't let them get away.'

'**Must not let them get away,**' Big Blob echoed. He moved more quickly, pounding across and

up the platforms, his giant body making it
easy for him to make it over each gap.

'He's catching up!' Joe warned.

Max stopped at a platform's edge. The next
platform was a moving one. It glided back
and forth in the air, too far away to reach at
the moment, but gradually getting closer.

'Come on, come on,' he whispered,
watching the platform floating towards him.

Max let out a **SCREAM** when he felt a jolt
of movement behind him, then turned to see
Gloop standing there. There wasn't enough
room for all three of them on this platform,
and Joe was still one behind. Big Blob was
quickly closing in. There was no way they'd
all get across the moving platform before he
caught up.

'You two go on,' Joe told them, scanning the platforms around them with his glasses. 'I'll find another way up.'

Max and Gloop both watched in **HORROR** as Joe jumped off the platform. They let out sighs of relief when he landed on another platform on the level below, and quickly began working his way up again.

'Max, the platform!' Gloop cried. Max turned and saw the moving platform had reached them, and was now moving away again.

'We'll never reach it!' said Max.

'Wait, what's that?' asked Gloop, pointing to a little ball of light floating in the air above them.

Max squinted at the thing, then let out

a **YELP** of delight. 'It's a power-up! They appear randomly in this level. But it's too far away.'

'For you, maybe,' said Gloop, and he jerked his **gooey** head hook towards the glow. It wrapped around the floating ball like a whip, then snapped it back towards them.

'What does it do?' Gloop asked, turning the ball over and over in his hands.

'I don't know,' said Max. 'It's random.' He looked back over his shoulder. Big Blob was almost on them now, and the platform was way beyond their reach.

'Oh well,' said Gloop. He pushed the ball into his **slimy** body. 'Let's find out.'

A glow lit up around Gloop, making him shimmer. There was a boing sound, and four large springs popped out from where his feet would be, if he had any.

'Grab on, Max!' Gloop cried.

And then, he jumped.

CHAPTER SEVEN

ACROBATIC ATTACK

Meanwhile, far below, Captain Crust was having problems of his own. Glitter Chick, Scampy, and Sugar Paws had been dazed after they'd all hit the ground, but now they were back on their feet, and had rushed to join Squeaky, who was not happy about the **slime**-ball he'd almost choked on.

There were four **Sicklies** and just one Captain Crust, and the old Goozilla's reflexes weren't what they used to be. Even with his ***SNOTSHOOTER***, he'd be lucky to take out one of them before the others reached him.

When Gunk and Atishoo had splatted down nearby, he'd hoped they'd help him, but having fallen from such a great height, it was taking them some time to pull themselves back together. He was on his own.

'Stay right where you are, you villains,' the captain warned. 'Don't come any closer.'

'Or what?' grunted Glitter Chick.

'Yeah,' chirped Squeaky Guinea Pig. 'What you going to do about it, old man?'

As one, the villains began to advance.

Max and Gloop sailed through the air towards the moving platform, holding onto each other. 'We're going to make it! We're going to make it!' Gloop cheered.

He landed on the platform, but the springs boinged again, launching them onwards and upwards. This time, they flew over three platforms, before rebounding off a fourth and flying into the air again.

'Whaaaaat are you doooooing?' Max howled, as Gloop bounced off a square of stone and hurtled upwards. 'Stooooop!'

'I can't!' Gloop cried, just as the

glow faded and the springs disappeared. He looked down. 'Huh? It wore off,' he muttered, before gravity took hold and they fell, just short of another ledge. Max grabbed for the platform, and his fingertips just managed to catch hold of the edge. He jolted to a stop, his legs swinging out beneath him as Gloop frantically tried to grab onto him.

'Don't let go, Max!' Gloop yelped, clinging tightly to Max's feet.

'I didn't plan to!' Max said.

'And don't look down!' Gloop warned.

'I won't! That would be crazy!' Max agreed.

He looked down. He couldn't help himself. He regretted it immediately.

'Ooh, this is high,' he squeaked, then he

cried out in fright as something
large and green and angry
landed on the platform they
clung to.

Big Blob turned slowly and
peered down at Max. His eyes
were still swirling, his face all
twisted up in anger.
'Must destroy Max,'
Blob said. **'Must destroy
Goozillas.'**

'S-snap out of it, Blob,'
said Max. 'We're
your friends,
remember?'

'**MusT desTroy,**' said Big Blob, his eyes spinning *FASTER* and *FASTER*.

Down at his feet, Max felt Gloop start to move. At first, he thought his friend was falling, but then he realized the Goozilla was wrapping his **slimy** head hook around Max's feet. The hook stretched out like a rubber band until Gloop was dangling several metres below Max's legs.

Max **GASPED** and tightened his grip as Gloop began to swing himself back and forth. 'What are you doing? We'll fall!' Max cried.

'Just hold on!' Gloop said. 'I've got an idea.'

Max gritted his teeth and tried to force all his strength into his fingers as Gloop

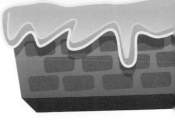

swung them both backwards
and forwards, building up
speed. Each swing made Gloop's head hook
stretch out, until he was swinging like a
trapeze artist at a circus.

Big Blob shuffled closer to the edge. His
immense weight pressed down on Max's
fingers, and Max had to bite his tongue to
stop himself **SCREAMING**.

And then, with an elastic **TWANG**,
Gloop swung up and over the platform
behind Big Blob and *SLAMMED* into the
giant Goozilla's back.

Despite the *SPEED* of the swing
and the force of the impact, Gloop only
managed to move Big Blob a centimetre or
so. Fortunately, it was just enough.

With a grunt of confusion, Big Blob lost his balance and toppled forwards over the edge. His hands grabbed for Max as he **PLUNGED** past him, eyes still spinning.

Down below, Captain Crust swept his **SNOTSHOOTER** across the approaching Sicklies. 'I'm w-warning you. Stay back,' he wheezed. He squeezed the cane's trigger, but the ball of snot missed its target and plopped against the ground a long way behind the Sicklies.

He fired again. This time, the shot whizzed harmlessly past Glitter Chick.

'Nice shooting, old man,' sniggered the wicked chicken. She pointed a stumpy wing at the captain. 'Get him!' she roared.

Captain Crust raised his cane to fire again, just as the world's largest Goozilla hit the ground with a **SPLUT** that shook the whole volcano. The shudder sent the captain's shot even wider than before. He and the Sicklies all watched as the spinning ball of snot shot upwards, bounced off first one platform, then another, before rebounding straight down towards Glitter Chick's feathery head.

The snot-ball exploded, spraying the Sicklies with a layer of gloopy green ooze.

'Let that be a lesson to you!' Captain Crust said. 'There's plenty more where that came from!'

'Yes!' cried Joe, watching events from his own platform. Gloop and Max had made it to safety, and were already chasing after Bubble Kitten. The cat still had a head start, but taking that wrong turning had cost her a lot of time. All it would take was for her to make one more slip-up and the Goozillas could still reach the **GLOB** piece.

Joe was about to join the chase again when something grabbed him from behind. A furry white paw spun him around, and Joe found himself staring into the wide eyes of Dreamy Bunny. Spirals spun and swirled in the bunny's eyes, and Joe felt a strange feeling of calm wash over him.

'HELLO, JOE,' she said. 'GAZE INTO THE EYES OF DREAMY BUNNY. YOU ARE NOW UNDER MY COMMAND . . .'

CHAPTER EIGHT

HYpNOTiZeD!

Thinking fast, Joe tapped a switch on his gadget glasses. The lenses clouded over, then became two shiny mirrors, reflecting Dreamy Bunny's gaze right back at her. The villain froze, her mouth hanging open, showing her two large front teeth.

'Now then,' said Joe, grinning broadly. 'You are under my command. And here's what I want you to do . . .'

Somewhere above, Gloop and Max were bounding and swinging from platform to platform, working together to close the gap on Bubble Kitten. They jumped the smaller gaps, and used Gloop's head hook to swing across the larger ones.

They landed side by side on a large metal platform with a little screen built into the floor. As soon as they touched down, the number three flashed up in red.

'What's this?' Gloop wondered. 'There aren't three of us.'

The number changed from three to two.

'That's more like it,' Gloop said.

'It's a countdown!' Max cried, grabbing hold of his friend as the countdown reached one. 'Jump!'

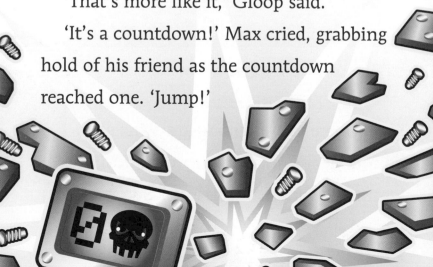

He and Gloop leaped to the next
platform, just as the one they'd jumped
from exploded. A moment later, it
reappeared, as if nothing had happened.

'Phew, that was close,'
Max wheezed.

'Exploding platforms?'
Gloop muttered.

'THAT'S JUST MEAN!'

'I know, but look, we're almost there!' Max said.

They were definitely catching up with the villainous kitty, and the piece of the **GOLDEN GLOB** wasn't far away. Max could see it up there, floating in mid-air below the opening that led to **CRUSTY CRATER**. There was just one problem.

'We're not going to make it,' he realized.

And he was right. Bubble Kitten was still too far ahead. She had to make just two or three jumps and the **GLOB** piece would be hers. There was no way for Max and Gloop to reach it in time.

Bubble Kitten had realized the same thing. She **CACKLED** as she flipped from one platform to the next, and smiled down at Max and Gloop below. 'Oh, so close,' she taunted. 'You made it all this way, only to fall at the final hurdle. **OUCH!** That must hurt.'

She paused on the platform she was standing on, and let out a **PURR** of triumph. 'You'll never be able to repair your precious **GOLDEN GLOB** now, which means this volcano of yours will be mine for the taking!'

Max felt his stomach tighten. Bubble Kitten was right. Even though the Goozillas had managed to get four **GLOB** pieces so far, Bubble Kitten only needed to get her paws on one to stop them bringing the **slime** back to the **WORLD OF SLIME**. Without the **slime**, the Goozillas would all dry out like Captain Crust. Max didn't want to think what would happen to them after that.

'You'll never get away with this, Bubble Kitten,' he warned. 'We'll stop you.'

The cruel kitty sneered, showing her teeth. 'Well, good luck with that,' she said. 'Now, anything you'd like to say before I get the **GLOB** piece and doom your **gooey** little chums forever?'

'I've got something to say,' said Gloop. Max and Bubble Kitten both looked at him.

'Yes?' purred the villainous feline.

Gloop grinned. 'Duck,' he said, just as

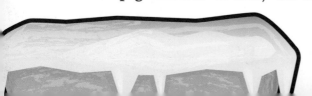

something white and fluffy slammed into Bubble Kitten from behind.

'No, wait,' said Gloop, as Bubble Kitten toppled over the platform's edge. 'It's not a duck. It's a bunny.'

Bubble Kitten landed on another platform, bounced, then rolled off the edge. Her claws scraped and scratched across the smooth surface as she tried to hang on.

With a **BOING**, Dreamy Bunny bounced down onto Bubble Kitten's platform. **'Must stop Bubble Kitten,'** she mumbled.

Max and Gloop exchanged a confused look. 'Huh? Why's she acting like that?' Max wondered.

'**Joe is the greatest,**' Dreamy Bunny continued. '**Joe is the most awesome Goozilla who ever lived.**'

Gloop giggled. 'I think that answers that question!'

'Come on, what are we waiting for?' said Max, grabbing Gloop by the arm. 'Let's get that **GLOB** piece!'

Down on the ground, Captain Crust breathed a sigh of relief as Big Blob heaved himself upright. 'Thank goodness. Just in the nick of time. I owe you one, Big Blob.'

Blob's eyes swirled around and around. **'Must destroy Goozillas,'** Blob intoned, as he slimed over to join the **Sicklies.**

'Yes, let's destroy the Goozillas,' said Scampy Hamster. They all fixed Captain Crust with wicked glares.

'STARTING WITH THIS ONE!'

CHAPTER NINE

THE FINAL JUMP

Max and Gloop bounded up the final few platforms. The **GLOB** piece was just another two or three leaps away, but Bubble Kitten was back in the chase. She had leaped onto another platform and was approaching the **GLOB** piece from the opposite direction. This was going to be close!

Dreamy Bunny bounded after the evil kitten, but as she touched down on one of the platforms, it lit up with an electrical charge. All the bunny's fur stood on end and her eyes stopped swirling.

'Ow,' she whimpered, then she toppled over and landed on another platform several levels below.

'**NICE TRY, GOO-LOSERS!**' Bubble Kitten hissed. She **SOMERSAULTED** onto another platform, then immediately **BOUNCED** onto the next. She was neck and neck with Max and Gloop now, with just one platform to go. The **GOLDEN GLOB** piece was directly between them, but she was moving *FASTER*!

Then she stopped, skidding to a halt right at the edge of the final platform. Max and Gloop stopped, too. The **GLOB** piece floated in the air like a tiny sun, with no platforms around it. If they jumped, they might be able to reach it, but there would be nothing for them to land on.

Even though he should have learned his lesson last time, Max looked down. They were at the highest point of the chamber now, and the ground was a **LOOOOONG** way away. Max could just see Captain Crust. The old Goozilla was surrounded by Sicklies, and Big Blob seemed to be helping them. Gunk and Atishoo were still dazed from the fall. The captain was in trouble, and he was all on his own. They had to help him, and fast.

Max looked across at Bubble Kitten. She was peering at the **GLOB** piece, trying to work out how to get to it. Max clicked his fingers and let out a gasp.

'Of course!' he cried. 'It's another invisible platform! We can just jump across and get it.'

He bent his legs and got ready to leap, but Bubble Kitten had heard every word.

'AHA! YOU FOOL. You really should have kept that to yourself!' she said.

And with a single bound, she leaped towards the invisible platform . . .

. . . and then discovered there wasn't one.

'WAAAAARGH!' Bubble Kitten yelped, plunging through thin air as she frantically flapped her arms and tried to fly. She fell, **SCREAMING**, for several seconds, then hit another platform. Max grinned and waved at her.

'Oops!' he said. 'I forgot. They're only invisible when you're standing on them.'

He and Gloop exchanged a high-five, then Max held onto his friend while Gloop whipped his head forwards. The **gooey** hook wrapped around the **GLOB** piece and snapped it back towards them.

'**NOOOOOO!**' howled Bubble Kitten, as Gloop held the piece of the **GOLDEN GLOB** above his head in triumph. 'Not again!'

Gloop lowered the shiny shard and was about to squidge it into his insides for safe keeping, when Max stopped him.

'Wait!' Max said. 'The **GLOB** pieces have given the others power-ups when they've absorbed them before, right?'

'Right!' Gloop said. 'I can't wait to see what sort of power-up I get!'

Max pointed downwards. 'I think someone else might need it more.'

Far below, Captain Crust was retreating.

His dried-out body moved slowly, and his voice came out like a whisper as he ordered the villains and Big Blob to stay back. 'I'm warning you. You chaps don't w-want to mess with m-me!'

'Look out below!' called Max.

Captain Crust leaned back and looked up, just as something golden and glowing fell towards him. The **GLOB** piece hit him right between the eyes, then sunk slowly down into his crusty old frame.

For a moment, the Captain's whole body lit up from the inside. His eyes came into focus again, and his moustache began to bristle. Snapping himself to attention, he tucked his cane beneath one arm, opened his mouth, and roared.

'ATTENNNNN-TION!'

Captain Crust's voice rolled out of him like a hurricane. It made the walls tremble and shook the floor, then the force of it slammed into the **Sicklies**, knocking them off their feet. Even Big Blob was staggered by it, and stumbled back a few metres.

The swirling in the giant Goozilla's eyes slowed down. With Dreamy Bunny now lying in a heap on a platform, her hypnosis powers had started to wear off.

'Pull yourself together, Big Blob!' the captain boomed. 'That's an order! Are you a Sicklie or are you a **GOOZILLA**?'

Big Blob frowned, confused by the question. The more he concentrated on the answer, the slower the swirling in his eyes became, until it was replaced by his usual puzzled stare.

'A Goozilla,' he said. 'I think.'

'That you are, Big Blob. That you are!' Captain Crust laughed. He turned to the Sicklies, just as they started getting back to their feet. 'All of you, drop and give me fifty, right now!' Captain Crust roared.

The Sicklies hesitated, but when the captain roared at them again, they all fell forwards onto their fronts and began doing push-ups. It wasn't hypnosis, exactly, but none of them dared disobey the captain's commands—especially now that Big Blob was standing over them, glaring down.

Groaning, Gunk shuffled over to join the others. Atishoo was perched on his head.

'What h-happened?' Atishoo asked, giving himself a shake. 'I can't remember a thing.'

'Sorry,' said Gunk, looking a little embarrassed. 'It took a while for me to pull myself back together. What did we miss?'

'Oh, don't you worry,' said the captain. He looked up and fired off a salute to Max and Gloop, who had been joined by Joe. 'Nothing I couldn't handle.'

CHAPTER TEN

THE LEAP HOME

A few minutes later, Max, Gloop, and Joe joined the others down on solid ground. The **SicKLies** were grunting and whimpering as they struggled their way through their fifty push-ups, under Big Blob's watchful gaze.

'Well, we did it again!' said Gloop. 'Five **GLOB** pieces collected, which leaves just one more to go.'

'Where's the last piece?' Max asked.

Joe pointed up towards the narrow hole in the ceiling, and the sky beyond. 'Up there.'

Max blinked. 'What? But we've just climbed all the way down from there! We could have gone through and got it!'

Gloop smiled sadly. 'No time, I'm afraid,' he said, just as the familiar sound of Max's screen time alarm rang out. His time in the **WORLD OF SLIME** was over for another day.

'Argh. I have to go,' he said.

'Indeed you do,' said Captain Crust. 'But we shall be waiting for you to return, and then we'll make the final assault on that last **GLOB** piece. Together.'

Max looked up. Bubble Kitten was leaning over the edge of the platform she had landed on. The only platforms around her were electrically charged ones, and a floating block above her meant she couldn't fly to safety in one of her bubbles.

'Um . . . could someone get me down?'

113

she cried. 'I think I'm stuck.'

Max grinned. He looked at the Goozillas and nodded. 'We'll get the **GLOB** piece together,' he agreed, then the world went all squidgy around the edges, and with a sudden jolt, he found himself back on his bed.

On the tablet's screen, a little egg-timer appeared over the **WORLD OF SLIME** icon. Max wouldn't be able to open it again until tomorrow. Luckily, his rumbling stomach told him just how to fill the time.

Bounding down the stairs, Max ran into the kitchen and was met by the smell of baking. 'Mmm. Are the cakes ready?' he asked.

'Yep!' said Amy, holding up a plate and

proudly displaying her creations.

Max's jaw dropped. Just as he'd expected, the cakes were decorated with pictures of some of Amy's favourite characters. These ones weren't dolls or princesses, though. They were something even worse.

'They're **World of Pets** cakes!' Amy announced.

She took a single cake from the plate and held it out towards Max, while beckoning with the other hand. 'I'll swap you one for the tablet,' she said.

Max shrugged and handed her the tablet. He took the cake and looked at the picture. Dreamy Bunny stared back at him from on top of the layer of purple icing. Max licked his lips, opened his mouth, and bit the cake in half.

'Mmm,' he said. 'Mesmerizing!'

'Hey! What happened to Bubble Kitten?' asked Amy, peering at the World of Pets icon on the tablet.

Max leaned over and looked at the screen. Bubble Kitten's fur was standing on end, and smoking slightly. It looked like she'd tried her luck with those electric platforms, after all.

'I'm not sure,' said Max, smirking. 'But she looks shocking!' And with that, he grabbed another cake, raced up the stairs, and began counting the hours until he could return to the **WORLD OF SLIME**.

JOIN MAX AND THE GOOZILLAS ON THEIR OTHER ADVENTURES IN THE
WORLD OF SLIME